SPIKS

SPIKS

Stories by
Pedro Juan Soto

Translated and with an Introduction
by Victoria Ortiz

Monthly Review Press
New York

Originally published by Editorial Cultural, Inc.,
Río Piedras, Puerto Rico, copyright © 1970
by Pedro Juan Soto

Library of Congress Catalog in Publication Data
Soto, Pedro Juan.
  Spiks.
  Short stories.
  I. Title.
PZ3.S718Sp [PQ7297.S64]   863   73-8057
ISBN 0-85345-299-7

Manufactured in the United States of America

10   9   8   7   6   5   4   3

Contents

To Rosiña, Manolo, and Roberto

I am no one:
a man with a shout of tar in my throat
and a drop of asphalt in my retina.

From "Perhaps My Name is Jonas,"
by Léon Felipe

Introduction by
Victoria Ortiz

During the end of the nineteenth and beginning of the twentieth centuries, Puerto Rican letters, like those of much of Latin America, passed through a phase of cultivated *costumbrismo*, a phase heavily influenced by and transparently derivative of Spanish literature. But in the late 1940s and early 1950s a group of young authors emerged who rapidly did away with many of the old modes and traditional styles, and initiated what was in fact a revolution in the field of the short story. This group, whose major contributors are Pedro Juan Soto, Emilio Díaz Valcárcel, René Marqués, José Luis González, Luis Rafael Sánchez, and Abelardo Díaz Alfaro, is loosely classified as the Generation of 1940, and has continued to enrich Puerto Rican letters ever since. The subjects which they opened up for the writer, and the innovative techniques which they developed, have clearly changed the total character of the contemporary Puerto Rican narrative.

It is not surprising that it should have been in the decades of the forties and fifties that this revolution began. The young authors, then in their thirties, were the first generation of Puerto Ricans to experience the *full* impact of United States domination. Although the United States had been in Puerto Rico since the beginning of the century, it was in 1916, shortly before any of these writers was born, that U.S. citizenship was imposed on all Puerto Ricans, and these men were among the first babies to be born "American." Their

11

early years coincided with the growth of the independence movement, and most of them were adolescents when the Nationalist militant Pedro Albizu Campos was imprisoned for the first time, accused of plotting to overthrow the United States government. They were the second generation of Puerto Rican schoolchildren to be taught entirely in English in the public schools (it was not until 1949 that Spanish was officially allowed once more to be the national language of the Puerto Rican people). Many of them, furthermore, spent the first years of their young manhood in the United States armed forces, and some of them fought in the Korean War. Most of these men visited New York in their youth, and several of them pursued their university studies "on the mainland," while others went there to live and work, and often to teach.

Thus, the Generation of 1940 knew, directly and indirectly, the turmoil of Puerto Rico's early years under United States rule, and in their adulthood they knew the years of benevolent imperialism which have so successfully clothed the iron fist in velvet. These historical influences have distinctly affected their work as writers. With them, a new literary language was born, showing the signs of an intense struggle to recapture something which had been taken from them. The Spanish peculiar to Puerto Rico—Caribbean in spirit, with traces of archaic peninsular Castilian and popular African vernacular, and increasingly incorporating English words and syntax—was consciously crafted by these writers, who clearly sensed an urgency not only to reestablish their mother tongue, but also to create new and more exciting forms. As they sought to break away from traditional literary influences, they also rejected conventional linguistic tenets and cultivated the transcription of regional and popular speech. These writers also searched for new subject matter and new approaches to popular themes. Their predecessors had frequently focused on the customs of the island's people, but had all too often produced quaint, one-dimensional characters viewed by an outside observer. The new generation turned to its people with a sense of comprehension and sharing, and with a profound interest in their characters' psychological rather than "picturesque" aspects. Their observations of daily Puerto Rican life, whether on the island or in the *metrópoli*, were strongly colored by a deep political awareness—often nonpartisan—which the turmoils of the 1930s, the reformism of the 1940s, and the war experience of the 1950s necessarily promoted. Often in spite of themselves, these authors produced vigorous political statements merely through a creative and realistic portrayal of protagonists continually confronting poverty, discrimination, and imperialism.

The major themes of the Generation of 1940 include life on the island under early United States domination, the imposition of English in the schools, and the incongruities of United States culture in the lives of the peasants. An important setting in their stories, and one which younger writers have also portrayed, is the Black and Puerto Rican ghetto of New York, where the advent of drug addiction and crime, and the sense of intense aloneness which characterizes New York life, are movingly probed. Those writers who fought in Korea have turned to that bitter experience, writing of the nightmare in the trenches and of the scars left on the bodies and spirits of the young Puerto Rican veterans and their families. The confrontations between United States imperialism and the independence struggles of the Puerto Ricans are frequent themes, set against the backdrop of industrialization on the island, the economic exploitation of its people, and the political commitment and militancy of the *independentistas*. In the work of all of these writers can be found the impact of this century's peculiar problems: alienation, political impotence, madness, and the rapidly changing social systems.

In their handling of these various themes, the Generation of 1940 reflects a confident step toward the redefinition of a national spirit, the reinstitution of familiar and appropriate world views, and the rejection of imposed and poorly digested alien structures. As such, their work most often emerges as a cry of despair, and there is little levity or humor in it. Their characters are tortured by real or imagined demons, twisted by agonies of mysterious origin; the worlds revealed are fraught with violence and tragedy, populated by grotesque and pathetic monsters; and the human interaction they depict is characterized by misunderstanding and cruelty, by victimization and brutalization.

One theme that distinguishes all of the narratives is the important—often dominant—role ascribed to the female characters. The writers of the Generation of 1940 take the Puerto Rican woman out of the mists of romanticism and mystery and place her full-blooded and human in the pages of some of their best stories. Seeing her and her role with new eyes, they have examined her intimate nature, her exchanges with others, and her social and human potential. The results are artistically intriguing and socially encouraging, for more directly than most national literatures in Latin America, the Puerto Rican has begun to come to terms with the realities of woman's existence, and has displayed a serious desire to understand her and her situation. While reared for passivity and dependence, the Puerto Rican woman has frequently been thrust into a life which requires precisely the opposite qualities. Given the amount of desertion by husbands and fathers, given the harshness of poverty, given the radical changes in family and social structure over the past few decades, the life of the Puerto Rican woman has in fact obliged her to be strong, independent, inventive, aggressive, and rational. Ironically, she has all too often reared her daughters for the unreal life. Raised for one role, forced into another—this is the contradiction which emerges from the stories of the Generation of 1940.

This is certainly true for Pedro Juan Soto's stories. In four of the six stories contained in this collection, a woman or women are the focal points of the action, as active doers, as causes, as motive forces. All of Soto's female characters express the anguish of the girl in the first story, "The Captive"; they are all captives, fighting, often blindly, to break out of the suffocating enclosures in which family and society hold them. Through these narratives we can watch the groping of women in their traditional roles of daughter, sister, wife, mother, and mistress; in all of them Soto leaves us feeling how poorly the roles are suited to the women. Although Fernanda, Hortensia, Altagracia, Graciela, and Nena will remain locked into the lives which torment them so, their

malaise and distress, their frantic, often harsh, always disas-
trous attempts to escape underline their strengths rather than
their weaknesses.

Pedro Juan Soto is in all ways a worthy representative of his
generation, sharing with the other writers many of the same
concerns and predilections, while at the same time cultivating
a narrative which is uniquely his own. Born in Puerto Rico in
1928, he moved at eighteen to New York where he went to
college, supporting himself in part as mail carrier, movie
usher, bus boy, and reporter for a Spanish-language newspaper. Upon graduation, Soto was drafted into the United States
army.

His experience in New York, where he lived for a total of
ten years, and his response to the Korean War provided some
of his earliest settings and themes. The first published stories
centered around Puerto Ricans in New York, and two of his
New York stories were awarded prizes by the Ateneo
Puertorriqueño: "Scribbles" in 1953 and "The Innocents" in
1954. In 1956 Soto published his first collection of New York
stories, *Spiks*. By then he was not only well known, but was
seriously challenging the older members of his generation
with his innovative use of language and his original themes.

Life in New York also served as the backdrop for Soto's
first novel, *Los perros anónimos* (*Anonymous Dogs*), in which the
Korean theme appeared for the first time. This work is,
unfortunately, still hidden at the back of one of the author's
filing cabinets, and he refers to it only casually. It was his
second novel, which won Outstanding Mention from the
Ateneo in 1958, that brought Soto the novelist to the
Spanish-reading public. In *Usmaíl* (a play on the words "U.S.

Mail"), we share the horror and fear of life on Vieques, an island off Puerto Rico which was in the past a peaceful agricultural community but is now a United States naval base where military maneuvers are carelessly and tragically carried out and the local population is left to fend for itself.

Pedro Juan Soto has also written for the theater, beginning his career as playwright with the prize-winning one-act play *El huésped* (*The Guest*), which recaptures his New York days. He has written other plays and a novel, *Ardiente suelo, fría estación*, which was published in translation early in 1973 as *Hot Land, Cold Season*. A more recent novel, *Temporada de duendes* (*Season of Gnomes*), has not yet appeared in English.

In all his work Pedro Juan Soto brings his readers or viewers a world sparingly drawn. He depicts scenes, characters, situations with a few quick, carefully planned strokes, devoid of unessential elaboration. The author rarely intrudes himself, rather permitting his striking though often painfully inarticulate characters to speak for themselves. In the stories collected in *Spiks*, Soto has transferred to paper the essence of Puerto Rican life in the hostile atmosphere of New York City. The reader can see the wintry, slushy streets of Spanish Harlem, the garbage-strewn empty lots of the South Bronx, the darkened hallways, peeling walls, dank basements, and communal toilets of the tenements in which his characters are forced to live. In these inhumane surroundings, his protagonists struggle and love and fail and endure with will and violence and passion; they often end in madness, self-delusion, or despair, but not before striking out against whatever has oppressed them.

SPIKS

Captive

In the distance she made out the taxi's red hood, focused on it, and followed it along the curve where the damp green of the gardens gleamed in the sun, bringing her gaze to the front bumper and from there to the building's entrance. The door on the left opened . . . and it was not he. A repulsive body—so small, so wretched, so different from his—crossed the entrance carrying a suitcase and went up the sloping passageway leading to the waiting room.

He won't come, she thought. *He was happy with a little hand squeeze on the porch, always worried about Inés and mama's eyes. Bastard. Coward. No . . . Probably Inés, without even realizing, keeps him tied down with all her errands: Baby, I need garlic. Tomatoes, baby. Baby . . . And I bet that little brat makes him think, too. Even if he loves me—and he does—he won't leave him. Coward. I can give him kids and a good home, bring him happiness damn Inés it would be a never-ending honeymoon he's mine Inés I can and if he really loves me—and he does, he does!* . . .

The glass wall reflected the wrinkled forehead under the ridiculous little felt hat, the watery eyes, and the tight lips (she had traced thick curves along those lips, forming a small heart), and she felt like beating her head against the glass and knocking down the old lady.

"Fernanda, I'm tired an I wanna siddown."

"So siddown. I aint stoppin you," she said, turning with

21

irritation toward the dyed-haired old woman, uncomfortably stiff in her narrow-waisted floral-print suit.

"Ay virgen, que tú . . . Fernanda, I tol you not to cry no more. People's gonna notice."

"Lemme alone," she mumbled, wiping her right eye with her fingers.

The loudspeaker roared: "Su atención, por favor. Llamada telefónica para Aníbal Montero. Señor Aníbal Montero, favor de acudir al mostrador de la Pan American . . . Your attention, please. Telephone call for Aníbal Montero . . ."

She turned because she no longer wanted to go on hunting taxis. She needed to forget him and the time that was passing so slowly.

Passengers wandered among the benches on both sides of the waiting room—not wanting to sit down so as not to wrinkle the uniforms of excitement they wore over their travel outfits—or entertained themselves collecting leaflets and pamphlets from the airlines, or sat inside the booth near the door posing for four-for-a-quarter snapshots, or took the children to ride those horses: a dime didn't make them bite or kick or whinny, but did make their rusted parts squeak each time they rotated on their sweated tubing.

Everyone was involved in killing swarms of minutes, like people swatting flies in a fish market.

Not wanting to imitate them, she turned her back again. She stopped another taxi with a glance and did not see him get out of this one either.

"Fernanda, I'm watchin you," said the old woman as she slyly scratched her back on the wall. "No sense goin on waitin

for him, he wont come. I tol him las night that if he comes
I'll go tell Inés all about it."

Her glance moved to the left and blazed like a torch against
the desolate, pitted old face.

"I dunno what you can be thinkin," protested the old
woman. "What you did was terrible an you wait an see, God'll
punish you. I aint said nothin to Inés cause she'll throw him
out and be bitter an alone. I aint worried bout him. He aint
worth nothin."

"Okay, okay," she said, reviving. "You can say its over for
now. But I got hopes . . ."

"You tryin to say that if he comes fer you . . . ?"

"I dunno."

"He's a good fer nothin, Fernanda. Jus let Inés catch him
with someone else."

"Wasn' his fault."

"So now yer defendin him," the old woman whispered,
looking obliquely at a man who walked by whistling. "If he
was a decent man . . . He don' respect the home where we
was all together, or my gray hairs or Inés or you. His wife in
the hospital givin birth an him in yer room, Fernanda . . ."

"I use to hear em at night," she said, following another
taxi. "Even tho I'd go to bed early, I'd stay up to hear
em . . ."

"To hear em?"

". . . but in the las months she didn' wanna so I . . ."

"Dios mío, Fernanda. Yer own sister . . ."

Without looking at the old woman, she took her
handkerchief from her bag and, wiping away the resignation
which framed her eyes, said: "I'm leavin, ain I?"

It was then that she saw him get out of a taxi, pay the driver, and slowly enter the building. She did not know what to do. *If mama sees him* . . . , she thought. She started walking toward the back of the hall. *Don't let him face mama now. Let him wait.*

"Where you goin?" asked the old woman, following her. "Yuh wanna siddown? I'm tired too."

"But waddabout this bench here, Fernanda?"

She pretended not to hear. Without excusing herself, she burst through a circle of four men: four festive faces, four pairs of baggy trousers, something about "the sweet life of Saturdays," and a distracted hand twirling a watch chain in the clamorous air.

Slumping on the empty bench, her back to the doors, she took off her shoes. *Aléjalo un poquito, San Alejo. Please God, let him stay away until mama leaves me alone.*

"Watsa matter?"

"There aint so many people here an I can take off my shoes."

"That don' look good," said the old woman, sitting down beside her.

"Nothin I do looks good."

Has he seen me? she thought. *He must be standing by the entrance looking for me.* She put her shoes on again, stood up, turned, brought her hand to her forehead, and closed her eyes. He was looking at her from far off, very rigid, then he turned and went out. *Where you goin? Don' be so scared, she won' eat you.*

Her hands were trembling. Her heart was a furious whelp trapped in a bag.

"My head hurts. I'm gonna get some aspr . . ."

She avoided the two children who were running across the hall, caught the hem of her dress on an umbrella, bumped into a couple walking hand in hand, was stepped on by a pilot who was walking absorbed in his newspaper, and finally went through the door leading to the left wing of the building. Suddenly she stopped dead. He was watching her from the little terrace on the left, between the pools. Instinctively, her hand rose a bit to greet him or to signal for caution, and then she looked back toward the old woman advancing through the crowd.

She returned to the door, placed a thick column as a wall before the old woman's eyes, and waited for her to come closer.

"Dios mío! These people don' let you walk."

"Buy me some asprins in the drugstore," she begged. "I feel too bad to go there."

The old woman looked around, like someone afraid of being stabbed in the back.

"You tryin to get rid of me, aint you?"

"I feel lousy. It aint what you think."

"The drugstore aint so far, Fernanda. Les both go."

"Aw, forget it, forget it," she said, and pushed through to the Pan American counter.

"Two-fifty-six still leavin on time?"

"Time's the same," said the employee. "Twelve five."

"Thanks."

She moved to one side, turned her body toward the door, and leaned an elbow on the counter. Her mother stood in front of her, reading the timetable on the other side of the counter.

"I'm just going to spend a whole month in Harlem," a

man, lanky and pompous, was saying to a youth scribbling in a notebook. "My work will be, you see, to investigate the conditions of Puerto Rican life in New York. I'd also like you to write . . ."

"Your attention, please," whined the voice through the loud-speaker system, sounding as if it were coming from beneath a rain of gravel. "Eastern Airlines announces the departure of Flight 364 to Miami. Please present your tickets at gate three. Su atención, por favor. La Eastern Airlines . . ."

Sunburned, self-important, carrying books and magazines under their arms, seven passengers moved toward gate number three.

The old woman shifted her weight from one foot to the other, breathed heavily, worried that no passing hand should brush her hip, while Fernanda, without seeming to, watched the glass wall giving out onto the terrace. Now he was hidden behind a column; she saw his hand holding his cigarette nonchalantly, and the brim of his hat. *Like in the movies,* she thought. *He's Alan Ladd, I'm Ava Gardner, and mama is Bela Lugosi. Cept that here Alan Ladd's hocked his gun.*

She began to laugh and did not stop until she noticed that the movements of her mouth and the stinging in her eyes had nothing to do with laughter.

"An now wha's wrong?"

"Nothin," she was able to stammer. "Just a joke."

"But you wanna cry again."

"It ain nothin, it ain nothin."

She took out her handkerchief, dried her eyes, and blew her nose. Then she went to sit on the bench closest to the door, her profile to the terrace. The old woman edged up to her.

"Why don' you go home? You mus have somethin to do."

"When the plane leaves," said the old woman.

"You wanna be sure, huh? But what more d'you want? It was you wrote to Julio tellin him I was gonna work."

"An live with them, Fernanda. Don' forget. I'll take care of checkin up that you aint gone to live alone."

"Or that I ain took the plane again for Puerto Rico."

"Or that you ain took the plane again for Puerto Rico. I'll be watchin every move you make."

"You want me to tell you bout my love affairs?"

"Julio will take care of you. That's what an older brother's for. The only thing I don' want is to see you here in Puerto Rico, not till everythin gets better."

"Better? Waddaya mean?"

"Till you grow up an realize what a sin you committed."

"An when'll I realize? When I'm twenny-one?"

"I hope so."

Four more years, she thought. *Then I can come fight for him. Take him away, marry him, if he hasn't already had the guts to leave Inés and come after me.*

"Tell Julio maybe I'll come see him at Christmas," said the old woman. "I wanna meet his wife and the two kids . . ."

She's not gonna leave me alone, she thought. *I'm not even gonna be able to kiss him.* Her glance paused on the posters—"Fly now, pay later." "Insure yourself for $25,000."—trying to ignore that jabbering mouth. Above the showcase of shell curios turned a sign with a neon aureola: "Tim's Shell Gifts . . . Tim's Shell Gifts . . . Tim's . . ."

She looked obliquely toward the terrace. He was still there, hidden like a gangster, viciously smoking away his caution. She crossed her legs. *Let him see them,* she thought. *Let him see what he's losing. Inés's are skinny. Inés aint got nothing like what I got. Except for him. But that was only luck, fast talk, and I was only a kid then with pimples and pigtails. But he didn't even mind that. He would send his looks out like hooks to rip my clothes down over my hips and my thighs. He was no fool, and me either.*

". . . And in New York you can get more for any secretary job than here," the old woman was saying.

"Uh huh."

"You gotta work hard, but you get good money. An when you know two languages . . ."

She began to hear the hoarse clamor of motors invading the waiting room as the voice reverberated: "Your attention, please. Pan American World Airways announces the arrival of Clipper Flight 216 from New York. Su atención, por favor . . ."

Speaking agitatedly, several people ran to look through the round openings giving out onto the landing strip.

". . . llegada del Clipper Vuelo dos dieciséis de Nueva York . . ."

She looked at her wristwatch. *Fifteen more minutes,* she thought. *Come on and kiss me. Mama won't say nothing. Have some guts. Come here, come here. You weren't reading the paper, you were talking to me with those devil eyes. Come here, you were saying. These hands, this mouth, and this are all gonna be yours. All that with your eyes, when you put down the paper and stretched in the armchair, stifling your yawn. Come here. Take this. Come here, your ma's in bed.*

"Fernanda."

"Waddaya want?"

"Aint you gonna eat nothin? On the plane I bet they don' give you nothin because everybody's eaten already."

"I ain hungry."

"Just a sanwich an a glass of milk."

"I don' want nothin."

In the waiting room, having given up their baggage for customs inspection, the passengers who had just come off the flight distributed kisses and embraces among mirthful friends and relatives.

"And when the snow falls, it's just like a Christmas card . . ." one man was saying.

"I aint gonna spend more'n six months here, because the countryside's turning into a backyard for all those factories they're building," said another.

She turned to look at a little boy who, fearfully and only at his mother's insistence, was caressing the flank of the wooden horse. The mother was talking to him, and the boy shook his head. *No, it's gonna hurt.* The mother went on talking affectionately, tousling his hair, stroking his cheek. *I don't dare because it'll hurt and anyhow you're my brother-in-law.* Finally the little boy allowed himself to be convinced. The woman picked him up, put him in the saddle, and put a coin in the slot. The horse began to jump, to turn, to rock . . . And it jumped, turned, and then rocked without dropping the trembling shout of the rider clinging to its neck.

She moved nervously on the bench. *It didn't hurt so much, but I would of like to have shouted with pain and pleasure.* She looked at the water in the first pool and, without raising her head, moving only her eyes, stared at the column. Now the cigarette smoke was all that betrayed his presence. *Coward, why don't you come here? Mama wouldn't say nothing. She's happy so long as I leave. What she can't forgive you for is coming out of my room when she was on her way back to bed after going to the bathroom. Write to me, coward. Think of me.*

"Your attention, please. Pan American World Airways announces the departure of Clipper Flight 256 to New York. Passengers will please present their tickets at gate seven."

A jumble of people lined up to pass through the turnstile to the observation deck. The little girls who had been primping in front of the mirror of the photo booth started running to whoever was calling them.

". . . anuncia la salida del Clipper Vuelo dos cincuentiséis con destino a Nueva York. Sírvanse presentar sus boletos en la puerta número siete."

The waiting room was now a track for the throng; laughing and weeping and shouting frenetically and scuffling hurriedly, they filed toward the gate.

The old woman pressed her lips on each of Fernanda's eyes, and she closed her mouth to brush it against her mother's fleshless cheek.

"God bless you, Fernanda. Qué Dios te bendiga. I'm gonna be upstairs on the observation deck."

When she saw her move away, she looked toward the terrace. But she could no longer make him out where she had last seen him. She looked around over the faces of strangers, and did not find him.

"Your ticket, please."

She handed over her ticket and once again looked for him.

"Excuse me, miss, but there are other passengers."

She started walking toward the landing strip, where a large cart full of baggage jolted and mechanics shouted. She walked up the stairs, turning her head toward the observation deck, and saw the old woman's handkerchief among the mass of arms and faces. She boarded the plane hurriedly, without answering the wave, and took a window seat. Her neighbor did not stop blowing kisses and waving his hand until the plane began to move.

The observation deck disappeared from sight, as did the entire rear facade of the building, and then the runway spread out before her. *Why didn't he come over when mama left me alone?* she thought. *One kiss would of been enough. Damn you, mama. If only you'd of gone . . .*

Suddenly, when the plane was turning slowly toward the control tower, a figure coming out onto the distant sidewalk caught her eye. It stopped—hands in pockets, tie in the wind, hat fluttering—and stared after the plane. *It's him! It's him!* Desperately, her hand waved a goodbye through the window. And he stood there with his head raised, his hat fluttering, his hands in his pockets . . .

You know I'm here, she thought. *Bend a little, even if you don't cry.* He pushed his chest out, steadied his legs. *Unless you don't care, unless you came just to be sure. Unless you came, like mama . . .*

The plane turned completely, sped down the runway, and took off. She began to laugh without wanting to, without effort. Soon the weeping came.

Miniature 1

Hey you, you talk English, you explain to this cop. That guy over there, well he was sittin there a long time with his pencil an paper, drawin ole drunk Minerva over there when she was dancin to the jukebox. An I went up behin him, see, to see how the picture was comin out an I didn' like it cause that aint Minerva he drawed. Look at the clean face . . . an she aint even got tits or a belly hangin down like Minerva's. Understand? An since he made such a doll out of such a beat up ole woman, I touched his shoulder and said: "Hey, kid, make me a picture of what I got down here." I didn' know he'd take it bad like that. A joke, see. The guy throws me a punch an me, well, I don' take that from no one but Marota, so I give it to him with a bottle. Tell the cop that guys like that, guys that don' know the scene . . . Aw, tell him it was self-defense!

Scribbles

The clock said seven and he woke up for a moment. His wife wasn't in bed and the children weren't on their cot. He buried his head under the pillow to close out the racket coming from the kitchen. He didn't open his eyes again until ten, forced to by Graciela's shaking.

He rubbed his small eyes and wiped away the bleariness, only to see his wife's broad body standing firmly in front of the bed in that defiant attitude. He heard her loud voice and it seemed to be coming directly from her navel.

"So? You figured you'd spend your whole life in bed? Looks like you're the one with a bad belly, but I'm carryin the kid."

He still didn't look at her face. He fixed his eyes on the swollen stomach, on the ball of flesh that daily grew and threatened to burst the robe's belt.

"Hurry and get up, you damned good-for-nothin! Or do you want me to throw water on you?"

He shouted at the open legs and the arms akimbo, the menacing stomach, the angry face: "I get up when I want to and not when you tell me. Hell! Who do you think you are?"

He turned his face back into the sheets and smelled the Brilliantine stains on the pillow and the stale sweat on the bedspread.

She felt overpowered by the man's inert mass: the silent threat of those still arms, the enormous lizard his body was.

Biting her lips, she drowned her reproaches and went back to the kitchen, leaving the room with the sputtering candle for Saint Lazarus on the dresser, the Holy Palm from last Palm Sunday and the religious prints hanging on the wall.

They lived in the basement. But even though they lived miserably, it was a roof over them. Even though overhead the other tenants stamped and swept, even though garbage rained through the cracks, she thanked her saints for having someplace to live. But Rosendo still didn't have a job. Not even the saints could find him one. Always in the clouds, more concerned with his own madness than with his family.

She felt she was going to cry. Nowadays she cried so easily. Thinking: *Holy God all I do is have kid after kid like a bitch and that man doesn't bother to look for work because he likes the government to support us by mail while he spends his time out there watching the four winds like Crazy John and saying he wants to be an artist.*

She stopped her sobs by gritting her teeth, closing off the complaints which struggled to become cries, returning sobs and complaints to the well of her nerves, where they would remain until hysteria opened them a path and transformed them into insults for her husband, or a spanking for the children, or a supplication to the Virgin of Succour.

She sat down at the table, watching her children run through the kitchen. Thinking of the Christmas tree they wouldn't have and the other children's toys that tomorrow hers would envy. Because tonight is Christmas Eve and tomorrow is Christmas.

"Now I shoot you and you fall down dead!"

The children were playing under the table.

"Children, don' make so much noise, *bendito!*"

"I'm Gene Autry!" said the oldest one.

"An I'm Palong Cassidy!"

"Children, I gotta headache, for God's sake . . ."

"You ain Palong Nobody! You the bad guy and I kill you!"

"No! Maaaaaaa!"

Graciela twisted her body and put her head under the table to see them fighting.

"Boys, geddup from under there! *Maldita sea mi vida.* What a life. ROSENDO, HURRY AND GET UP!"

The kids were running through the room again, one of them shouting and laughing, the other crying.

"ROSENDO!"

Rosendo drank his coffee and ignored his wife's insults.

"Waddaya figure on doin today, lookin for work or goin from store to store and from bar to bar drawin all those bums?"

He drank his breakfast coffee, biting his lips distractedly, smoking his last cigarette between sips. She circled the table, rubbing her hand over her belly to calm the movement of the fetus.

"I guess you'll go with those good-for-nothin friends of yours and gamble with some borrowed money, thinkin that manna's gonna fall from the sky today."

"Lemme alone, woman . . ."

"Yeah, its always the same: lemme alone. Tomorrow's Christmas and those kids ain gonna have no presents."

"Kings Day's in January . . ."

"Kings don' come to New York. Santa Claus comes to New York!"

"Well, anyhow, whoever comes, we'll see . . ."

"Holy Mother of God! What a father, my God! You only care about your scribbles. The artist! A grown man like you."

He left the table and went to the bedroom, tired of hearing the woman. He looked out the only window. All the snow that had fallen day after day was filthy. The cars had flattened and blackened it on the pavement. On the sidewalks it had been trampled and pissed on by men and dogs. The days were colder now that the snow was there, hostile, ugly, at home with misery. Denuded of all the innocence it had had the first day.

It was a murky street, under heavy air, on a grandiosely opaque day.

Rosendo went to the bureau and took a bundle of papers from the drawer. Sitting on the window sill, he began to examine them. There were all the paper bags he had collected to tear up and draw on. He drew at night, while the woman and children slept. From memory he drew the drunken faces, the anguished faces of the people of Harlem: everything seen and shared during his daytime wanderings.

Graciela said he was in his second childhood. If he spent time away from the grumbling woman and the crying children, exploring absentmindedly in his penciled sketches, the woman muttered and sneered.

Tomorrow was Christmas and she was worried because the children wouldn't have presents. She didn't know that this afternoon he would collect ten dollars for the sign he painted yesterday at the corner bar. He was saving that surprise for

Graciela. Like he was saving the surprise about her present.

For Graciela he would paint a picture. A picture that would summarize their life together, in the midst of deprivation and frustration. A painting with a melancholy similarity to those photographs taken at saints' day parties in Bayamón. The photographs from the days of their engagement, part of the family's album of memories: they were both leaning against a high stool, on the front of which were the words "Our Love" or "Forever Together." Behind was the backdrop with palm trees and the sea and a golden paper moon.

Graciela would certainly be pleased to know that in his memory nothing had died. Maybe afterward she wouldn't sneer at his efforts anymore.

Lacking materials, he would have to do the picture on a wall, and with charcoal. But it would be his, from his hands, made for her.

Into the building's boiler went all the old and useless wood the super collected. From there Rosendo took the charcoal he needed. Then he went through the basement looking for a wall. It couldn't be in the bedroom. Graciela wouldn't let him take down her prints and palms.

The kitchen wall was too cracked and grimy.

He had no choice but to use the bathroom. It was the only room left.

"If you need to go to the bathroom," he said to his wife, "wait or use the pot. I have to fix some pipes."

He closed the door and cleaned the wall of nails and spiders' webs. He sketched out his idea: a man on horseback, naked and muscled, leaning down to embrace a woman, also naked, wrapped in a mane of black hair from which the night bloomed.

Meticulously, patiently, he repeatedly retouched the parts that didn't satisfy him. After a few hours he decided to go out and get the ten dollars he was owed and buy a tree and toys for his children. On the way he'd get colored chalks at the candy store. This picture would have the sea, and palm trees, and the moon. Tomorrow was Christmas.

Graciela was coming and going in the basement, scolding the children, putting away the laundry, watching the lighted burners on the stove.

He put on his patched coat.

"I'm gonna get a tree for the kids. Don Pedro owes me ten bucks."

She smiled, thanking the saints for the miracle of the ten dollars.

That night he returned to the basement smelling of whiskey and beer. The children had already gone to sleep. He put up the tree in a corner of the kitchen and surrounded the trunk with presents.

He ate rice and fritters, without hunger, absorbed in what he would do later. From time to time he glanced at Graciela, looking for a smile that did not appear.

He moved the chipped coffee cup, put the chalk on the table, and looked in his pocket for the cigarette he didn't have.

"I erased all those drawins."

He forgot all about the cigarette.

"So now you're paintin filth?"

He dropped his smile into the abyss of reality.

"You don' have no more shame . . ."

His blood became cold water.

". . . makin yer children look at that filth, that indecency . . . I erased them and that's that and I don' want it to happen again."

He wanted to strike her but the desire was paralyzed in some part of his being, without reaching his arms, without becoming uncontrolled fury in his fists.

When he rose from the chair he felt all of him emptying out through his feet. All of him had been wiped out by a wet rag and her hands had squeezed him out of the world.

He went to the bathroom. Nothing of his remained. Only the nails, bent and rusted, returned to their holes. Only the spiders, returned to their spinning.

The wall was no more than the wide and clear gravestone of his dreams.

Miniature 2

There was four: Horti, Lucy, Sara, an Virginia. Almost like a dance program, see. An when we tell em that we can only have three cause Monchín's *aleluya,* he's a believer, Lucy says: "Daddy, tough fer you." We thought it was cute, I dunno. You know how it is. An then the warmin up: the beer, the smokes, the hands under the table. An Monchín sat there sorta snooty like (even the chachachas bothered him), but not sayin nothin. "Hey, Daddy, where's yours?" says Horti, an puts her hand there. Monchín wants to leave right away, but I stop him, sayin we'll go to the corner with him. Then he's walkin in front while we're feelin round ass an kissin lipstick an I fix it all up with Sara an the guys. You know how it is. Before we get to the corner, we push him in the alley an . plunk, down goes Sara. Sara was a octopus on top of him . . . I dunno. An Monchín puked. He didn' even have nothin to drink. An did he bawl! You know how it is. I dunno.

The Innocents

climb to the sun on that cloud with the pigeons without horses
without women and not smell when they burn the tin cans in the lot
without people to make fun of me

From the window, wearing the suit made and sold to fit the
man he was not, he saw the pigeons hovering under the eaves
across the way.

or with doors and windows always open to have wings

He began to flap his hands and make noises like the
pigeons when he heard the voice behind him.

"Baby, baby."

The shriveled woman was seated at the table (under it was
the flimsy suitcase fastened with rope, its only key), watching
him with intense eyes, sunk in her chair like a hungry and
abandoned cat.

"Pan," he said.

Giving it a light nudge away from the table, the woman
pushed the chair out and went to the cupboard. She got the
piece of bread that was lying exposed on the boxes of rice and
took it to the man, who was still gesticulating and mouthing
sounds.

to be a pigeon

"Don' make noise, Pipe."

He crumbled the piece of bread on the window sill without
paying attention to her.

"Don' make noise, baby."

41

The men playing dominoes under the store awning were looking up.

He stopped moving his tongue.

without people to make fun of me

"A pasiar a la plaza," he said.

"Yes. Hortensia's comin to take you for a walk."

"A la plaza."

"No, not to the plaza. They took it away. It flew away." He pouted. He listened again to the fluttering of the pigeons.

"No, it wasn' the pigeons," she said. "It was the Evil One, the Devil."

"Ah."

"You have to pray to Papá Dios to bring back the plaza."

"Papá Dios," he said, looking outside. "Trai la plaza y el río . . ."

"No, no. Don' open yer mouth," she said. "Kneel down an talk to Papá Dios without openin yer mouth."

He knelt in front of the window, joined his hands and looked out over the roofs.

want to be a pigeon

She looked out below, at the idleness of the men on a Saturday morning and the briskness of the women hurrying to and from the market.

Slowly, sorrowfully, but erect, as if balancing a bundle on her head, she walked toward the room where her daughter, in front of the mirror, was taking the pins out of her hair and piling them on the bureau top.

"Don' take him today, Hortensia."

The younger woman glanced at her out of the corner of her eye.

"Don' start that again, mama. Nothin ain gonna happen to him. They'll take good care of him and it don' cost us nothin."

As it was freed from the pins, her hair fell over her ears in a pile of tight curls.

"But I know how to take care of him. He's my boy. Who knows better than me?"

Hortensia studied the slight and slender figure in the mirror.

"Yer old, mama."

A fleshless hand appeared in the mirror.

"I ain dead yet. I can still take care of him."

"It ain that."

The curls were still tight, despite her attempts to loosen them with the comb.

"Pipe's innocent," said the mother, her words water for a sea of grief. "He's a baby."

Hortensia put the comb down. She took a pencil from the open bag on the dresser and began to blacken her scanty brows.

"You can't cure that," she said to the mirror. "You know it. Tha's why the best thing is . . ."

"In Puerto Rico this wouldn' of happened."

"In PR it was different," said Hortensia over her shoulder. "People knew him. He could go out because people knew him. But in New York people don' care and you don' even know yer neighbors. Life's tough. Its years an years I been sewin and sewin an I ain even married yet."

Looking for the lipstick, she saw her mother's face crumble in the mirror.

"But that ain the reason either. They can take better care of him there."

"Tha's what you say," said the mother.

Hortensia tossed the makeup and comb into her bag and closed it. She turned: flimsy blouse, gleaming lips, blackened eyebrows, tight curls.

"After a year here, we deserve somethin better."

"It ain his fault what happens to us."

"But its gonna be if he stays here. Jus look."

She darted at her mother, taking her arm and pushing up the short sleeve. On the loose upper arm was a purple blotch.

"He raised his hand to you already, an me in the factory I aint easy thinkin what could be happenin with you an him. An with this already . . ."

"He didn' mean it," said the mother, pulling her sleeve down and looking at the floor as she twisted her arm so that Hortensia would let go.

"He didn' mean it, with one hand on yer throat? If I hadn' of grabbed that bottle, God only knows. We ain gotta man aroun to stand up to him, an I'm turnin into a wreck an yer scared of him."

"He's a baby," said the mother in her docile voice, drawing into her body like a snail.

Hortensia half closed her eyes.

"Don' start with that again. I'm young an I got my life in fron of me an he ain. Yer tired too an if he wasn' here you could live better fer the years you got left an you know it but

you don' dare say it cause yer scared its wrong but I say it for
you *yer tired* an tha's why you signed those papers cause you
know that in that place they take better care of him an then
you can sit an watch the people go by in the street an when
you want you can get up an go out an walk aroun like them
but you'd rather think its a crime an that *I'm* the criminal so
you can be a martyred mother an *you bein a martyred mother*
can't deny that but you gotta think of yerself an me. Cause if
that horse threw him when he was ten . . ."

The mother left the room quickly, as if pushed, as if the
room itself blew her out, while Hortensia was saying:
". . . an the other twenny years he lived like that, sense-
less . . ."

She turned to watch her leave, without following, leaning
on the dresser where she now felt her fists hammering out a
beat for her near scream.

". . . we lived them with him."

In the mirror she caught sight of the hysterical carnival
mask that was her face.

*and there's no roosters and there's no dogs and there's no bells and
there's no river wind and there's no movie buzzer and the sun doesn't
come in here and I don't like*

"Enough," said the mother, bending over to brush the
crumbs off the sill. The throng of kids hit and chased a rubber
ball down the street.

and the cold sleeps sits walks here inside and I don't like it

"Enough, baby, enough. Say Amen."

"Amen."

She helped him get up and put his hat in his hand, seeing that Hortensia, serious and red-eyed, was coming toward them.

"Les go, Pipe. Give mama a kiss."

She put her bag on the table and bent down to pick up the suitcase. The mother threw herself on his neck—her hands like pliers—and kissed the burned hazelnut of a face, smoothing her fingers over the skin she had shaved that morning.

"Les go," said Hortensia, carrying bag and suitcase.

He wriggled out of his mother's arms and walked to the door, swinging the hand which carried the hat.

"Baby, put on yer hat," said the mother, and she blinked so that he would not see her tears.

Turning, he raised it and left it on top of his vaselined hair, so small it looked like a toy, as if it wanted to compensate for the waste of material in the suit.

"No, leave it here," said Hortensia.

Pipe pouted. The mother fixed her eyes on Hortensia and her chin trembled.

"Okay," said Hortensia, "carry it in yer hand."

He walked again to the door and his mother followed, hunching over a bit now and holding back the arms that wanted to stretch out toward him.

Hortensia stopped her.

"Mama, they're gonna take care of him."

"I don' want them to beat . . ."

"No. There's doctors. An you . . . every other week. I'll take you."

They both made an effort to keep their voices steady.

"Go lie down, mama."

"Tell him to stay there . . . not to make noise an to eat everythin."

"Yeah."

Hortensia opened the door and looked out to see if Pipe had stayed on the landing. He was amusing himself by spitting over the bannister and watching the saliva.

"I'll be home early, mama."

The mother stood next to the chair that was already superfluous, trying to see him through the body which blocked the entrance.

"Lie down, mama."

The mother did not answer. With her hands joined in front of her, she was rigid until her chest and her shoulders shook convulsively and the delicate and gulping sobbing began.

Hortensia pulled the door shut and went hurriedly downstairs with Pipe. Facing the immense clarity of a June midday, she longed for hurricanes and eclipses and snowfalls.

Miniature 3

It all happened because Chano, the guy who hacks nights between Harlem and the airport, had been swinging on one of the chairs in the barbershop and the boss told him to quit it. To the insults Chano threw at him, the barber answered with silence and a gesture that meant that words are easy prey for the wind.

And there was nothing else . . .

The barber left at four to cut the hair of the cripple in the building across the street, and Chano stopped him to shout more obscenities and to hit him twice with the fuckitall whip he kept in the taxi. The razor (did the barber take it out, or maybe the blows loosened his muscles, undoing the bundle in his hand?) drew an *x* across Chano's chest and belly. And the two strokes went whishwhash, whishwhash . . .

. . . Until they removed Chano's disemboweled body . . .

Absence

Altagracia secured the three locks on her apartment door and slip-slapped up the stairs to the third floor, to her mother's place, wearing a dirty and frayed robe over her thin body, and on her face a martyr's lassitude and anemia, her hair graying and loose over her ears.

Once upstairs, she pushed open the door that was never locked, except at night, and went panting into the kitchen, her mules clack-clacking along the hallway. In her listless and ravaged voice she greeted the breakfasting woman and dropped onto a chair. Her mother looked at her over her cup of coffee without saying anything, watching her come as always: rings under her eyes, defenseless, gaunt.

"You goin to the market?" asked Altagracia, drawing air into her lungs to calm her panting.

"Sure . . . like every Saturday, like it or not."

The mother took her last gulp and got up to heat the milk for Altagracia's coffee, annoyed at having to answer stupid questions so early.

"Why?" she asked, as she lit the burner. "Cancha help me today?"

"Ay, I feel so bad," Altagracia's voice sounded monotonous and tired. "Susana can help you . . ."

"Susana?" The mother put the steaming cup on the table. "Susana got in at all hours, from one of those dances she goes to . . . There's bread on the icebox if you want."

"Uh uh, leave it, I'm only gonna have some coffee. Wacha gonna do with that girl? All she does is get drunk an party aroun. Always with another fella . . ."

"Well. Tha's the style nowadays," said the mother. "Waddaya want me to do if tha's the style? In Puerto Rico, in my day you didn' see such things . . . an even today women watch out for themselves over there. But here even the papers write about it an make it look good. Its the style in New York . . ."

"Unless that girl gets married . . ." said Altagracia, and immediately voiced another concern. "Lupe call me up las night."

"Waddid she want?"

Not receiving an immediate reply, the mother stopped cleaning the burners and turned. Altagracia was slowly pouring three spoonfuls of sugar into her cup, absorbed in watching the grains fall.

"Waddid Lupe want?" insisted the mother.

"Nothin. Jus to offer me a job in the factory . . ."

"An waddid you tell her? Yes?"

"I tole her no."

Altagracia put the spoon on the saucer and took her first sip.

"But aincha gonna work no more? Its more than five years."

"I'm tired."

"But from what? I was workin till jus a while ago an I'm almos sixty . . ."

"Yeah, but I'm tired. S'there any cole water?"

"In the icebox." The mother turned her back so she would

not be obliged to get out the bottle Altagracia could reach from her chair. "Howdja sleep las night?"

"Like always. Bad."

Her daughter settled in her chair after watering her coffee, sipping it, and finding it to her taste.

"Wyncha go see a doctor bout not sleepin. Doctor Ruiz . . ."

"What I got," said Altagracia, angrily sweetening her coffee, "no doctor ain gonna cure. Its a spirit that follows me an doctors don' cure that . . ."

"A spirit? Whose?"

The mother had forgotten the dishes as she listened closely to the voice that hardly spoke above a whisper. Now she saw shadows and a glow in the room.

"Mario's."

"But, come on, yer husband aint . . . dead," said the mother. And she looked at the opposite wall, to which Altagracia was speaking as if she were seeing her husband face to face.

"That don' matter . . . He follows me even tho he's alive an faraway. He don' want me to see no one . . . specially no other men."

"But it was him left you . . ."

Intrigued, the mother moved closer and sat down on the edge of her chair.

"He's selfish," Altagracia said. "He don' want no one to love me. Las night he was in the apartment, walkin back an forth, an finally he came in my room an tole me he didn' wanna see me with no man."

"But you don' see no one. How long ago he leave? Three years?"

"Three an a half . . ."

"Well, an since then you don' even go out or have no fun . . . You don' even go to the movies . . ."

"Tha's how he wants it."

"Wha's happening is that you live alone, Altagracia. Its bad to always be alone."

"No, tha's how he wants it. He can't ferget me an tha's why he haunts me . . ."

"But if he loved you he wouldn' of joined up again after he got back from the war an said he didn' want nothin to do with uniforms no more."

"Its that there's somethin that separates us. But anyhow he loves me."

"He don' send you the checks no more, an he don' write."

"Tha's to test me," said Altagracia, still possessed, still talking to the wall because he was there, watching and hearing her.

"And wacha gonna do? Go on like that, without fixin yerself up none, alone, gettin old at thirty-two, older'n Susana an her older'n you?"

"He don' want me to get prettied up or see no one. After all, he's my husban!"

"An howd' you know that?"

"Cause he spoke to me in Don Geño's place, you know, the spiritist, an also in my room."

The mother was afraid. Her daughter spoke of terrible and inexplicable forces, of men with strange powers and hypnotic stares: sinister beings, vampires who could be banished only by showing them the cross and killed only by shooting them with a silver bullet.

God knows how that man has come to haunt the house, she thought. *He's gotta be dead to haunt the house like that. There's nothing worse in this world than men.*

"I'm goin home," said Altagracia, with a gesture of fatigue. And she touched her mother's hand, not noticing how the older woman shuddered. "I wanna lay down some . . ."

She rose slowly, without finishing her coffee, waiting for him to leave first and meet her downstairs, in front of her door. Then she walked down the hallway, filling it with the slip-slap of her mules and the odor of witch hazel.

The mother, rigid in her chair, crossed herself as soon as she heard the door slam. *These are bad times,* she thought. *A spirit chasing Altagracia. And her more and more like a mummy every day. She don't work. She lives and eats off us. And Susana never missing a party and drinking like a man and coming in at all hours, rowdy like a bewitched man. In spite of all those promises after my heart attack, when I told her not to kill me with grief.*

Altagracia triple-locked her door and admonished no one: "Wipe yer feet good . . . you always come in with dirty feet . . ."

She went to the living room, where the old furniture and the sale lamps and the unrecognizable photographs were neatly placed and gleaming, forming a dark, well-cared-for museum.

She opened the curtains to look out into the street and moved to one side as if she feared being seen from outside or was making room for somebody else.

It was one more spring day, sunny, gay. The street was filling up with the coming and going of women in garish dresses, with the idleness of men in the doorway of the pool hall, with the clutches of old women gossiping on the stoops, and with the music blaring from the record store.

"Look wadda nice day, Mario. A day to be outside, in the sun. But you always like to be closed in here, always behin me, never missin a step . . . No, I know you don' like to go out, you like to be in the house cause yer comfy. It don' bother me you bein here with me. Better here than in some bar, drinkin and fightin . . ."

She closed the curtain so that no more light could enter. His photograph stood out on the shelf with the novels by Delly: an enlargement of a snapshot taken at bootcamp.

"But the house also ends up bein borin. Aint much to do . . . only talk. I don' mean it that way, Mario. I like to talk . . . But you know, if we had a kid . . . Play with him, take care of him . . . I dunno. You need . . . Or even a daughter. Dress her up like a little doll, take her out fer a walk . . . A girl looking like me? Huh! . . ."

His face was blurred, fuzzy. If he hadn't signed it at the bottom she never would have known it was her husband.

"Pretty . . . Tha's what you tell me all the time. Jealous fer what? Ah, but it don' mean nothin if they look! You know I don' pay no attention to no one who aint you . . . You'd kill for me? For me? Ay, Mario, don' talk like that cause I don' like it . . . Course I'd like to have a little girl. An with a name like yours. Marisela! Somethin like that. Or . . . wait . . . once I read in a book . . . a story . . . Maria somethin . . . Maria . . . Marianela! Tha's better. I . . . No, now I

remember that Marianela was blind . . . or was it her
boyfriend . . . someone. No, we better not name her that. It
brings bad luck. Better make it Marisela . . . What?"

In the photograph, an arrogant stance: cap pushed back,
cigarette hanging from his mouth, arms crossed over his chest,
and his belly pushed forward, challenging.

"A drink? You startin already . . . It's bad so early . . .
Okay, there it is. In the kitchen . . . No, I aint gonna get it.
I aint gonna drink nothin."

She walked toward the kitchen, turning now and then to
gesticulate as she spoke.

"Yer jus like a kid, Mario. Gotta do everythin for you. I'll
give you one an no more."

The kitchen, another cave, was a storeroom for empty
flower vases, untouched utensils, tablecloths and napkins
yellowed from disuse, and rusty mousetraps which would
never again catch anything. She took the half-full whiskey
bottle from the cabinet and brought two glasses from the
shelf. She filled both and raised hers.

"No, not to me, to you . . . To you, Mario . . ."

She downed her glass, her head thrown back, breathing
with relief once she saw it empty and on the table once again.

"You won' mind if I tell you somethin? I needed that little
drink. I get up so tired . . . More'n when I go to bed. It's that
I don' sleep so good. You throw the covers off every now an
then, an I spend the night pullin them back on me. An I
think about all kindsa things . . . When we was courtin,
remember? We'd go to the Bronx, Central Park, Coney Islan
. . . It was good then . . ."

She poured more whiskey in her glass and sat at the table, looking at the chair in front of her.

"You don' wanna go out to no more parties cause you say I get mad. I don' get mad about goin to parties. Its jus that you start drinkin and so long as you drink a little its okay . . . till the fourth or fifth glass. Then, no. Then you start insultin people . . . But Mario, no one makes passes at me . . . No, yer jus too jealous . . ."

She tilted the glass again, feeling the fire rise and fall within her body. Guessing that the liquor, as always, would make her forget that only outside was there sun. Promising her the sun between those walls and even within herself.

"But how come you ask me that so much? You know I love you . . . I adore you . . . (*Singing.*) Que yo soy tuya na máh . . . I belong to only you . . . Ay . . . don' kiss me yet . . ."

She laughed nervously, as if she wanted to stop her laughter and could not, while her body contorted grotesquely.

"Its that yer ticklin me, baby . . . Course I love you. Naw, be good now . . . siddown, now we're gonna toast so we're always together."

She filled the glass once more and drank it more rapidly, almost in one gulp: it was she who poured herself into the liquid. She felt her cheeks burn and her eyes flame, and a marvelous languor spread through her body.

"I shouldn' drink so much, Mario . . . Yuh know I get so I'm even ashamed after. Yeah, I know, we're home . . . But . . . even if it's only with you that I do this . . . you look so hansome today. (*Singing and moving sensually.*) Un poquito de tu amol, un poquito nada más . . . Tha's the tie I gave you, ain it? It looks good on you . . . (*Singing again.*) Una mirada de tus ojoh . . . Ay, don' take it off. Keep yer tie on, baby, don' . . . Don' get undreeeessed . . . An what if someone knocks on the door? An if mama? Mario, noooo . . . Mario, noooo . . . be good . . ."

She closed her eyes and felt she was dizzy and drowning, but both feelings were delicious.

"Mario . . ."

Opening her eyes, she unknotted the belt of her robe. She let it fall to her feet and walked over it, naked, toward the bedroom. Her frail body, the color of old sulphur, straightened up voluptuously.

She threw herself down on the bed, moaning: "Mari-ooo . . ."

Waiting for him, moving her body and passing her thin hands over her meager breasts and flaccid thighs, she called: "Mariooo . . . Marioooo . . ."

Miniature 4

They were coming out of the hospital when the other man said, "And howd' ya feel now yer a father?"

"Pretty bad, thanks."

The first man laughed. "Well, I'd like to have one, but since Lola can't . . ."

They stopped to wait for the bus and the first man began to dig in his pockets. He threw two copper pennies in the stagnant gutter water.

"Whenever I find pennies in my pockets, its like the devil gets in me."

His hospital care, his doctor, his crib . . .

Two more pennies clinked on the sidewalk.

"Dirty pennies bring me bad luck."

. . . His food, his visits to the clinic, his illnesses, his winter clothes, his summer clothes . . .

"How come you so quiet?"

"Aw, shit, lemme alone!"

. . . His new apartment, his toys . . .

Bayaminiña

From the distance, if one went by its colors, it was a snappy little cart parked on the corner of 116th street. It had blue, red, and yellow stripes, and the box on top—full of cod fritters, blood sausage, and banana fritters—had glass on all four sides. From close, however, you could see that its snappiness was no more than a front that disguised the wear and tear and the rot which were consuming it from the wheels up to the push bar. On a piece of tin nailed to the front you could read in red, shaky letters: BAYAMINIÑA.

But no one paid attention to the cart. The crowd was watching the argument between the vendor and the policeman. The black women heading toward Lenox Avenue stopped in their rapid, ass-swinging tracks to see how it would all end. The customers in the nearby bar neglected their drinks and the TV set to follow the altercation through the glass window. And curiosity even turned heads in passing cars and busses.

"I pay no more," the vendor was saying, tense. "I pay las year other fine . . ."

The policeman only shook his head as he finished scribbling in his notebook.

"This has nothing to do with last year, buddy."

"I got no money. I no pay more."

"And the fine you'll have to pay next year will be a bigger one, if you don't get rid of that thing there."

"You're killing me," said the vendor. "Why you do this?"

"The Department of Health . . ."

"Okay, you gimme a job an I . . ."

". . . is after you guys."

"I have to eat," said the vendor. "Don't gimme no fine, gimme a job."

"I have nothing to do with that," said the policeman. He put the summons in one of the vendor's pockets and added: "You keep that . . . And remember to go to court."

The vendor took out the summons, furious, and tried to read it. But he could understand no more than the numbers.

"All right, break it up," the policeman said to the crowd. And to the vendor: "And you get going before I lose my patience."

The vendor turned to the school kids, slight and cinnamon-colored like him.

"These bastards," he said to them in Spanish. "Sia la madre d'ehtos policías!"

"C'mon," said the policeman. "Get the hell out of here."

Suddenly the vendor bent over, picked up the rock which served as the cart's brake, and stood up again with it in his fist. His face was already crumpling with a coming sob.

"Gimme a job, saramabich!"

"You'd better get your ass out of this neighborhood before I throw you in jail!" said the policeman, not raising his eyes from the threatening fist while moving his hand to his gun holster.

The vendor hesitated, grimaced angrily, turned, and threw himself on the cart. Crash! went the panes and crack! the wood. And he shrieked: "Gimme a job, saramabich, gimme a job!"

And the tin—clank! clank!—where you could still read BAYAMINIÑA, turned dirty with blood, spattered with tears, and, freed from its nails, once again became a tin can.

Miniature 5

In the classroom full of disheveled heads and skinny bodies, her porcelain face forced itself to hold together in the midst of shouting and grunts whose only language was mockery.

"As I was saying, today we'll study the sounds of English. Gorzia, what . . ."

Laughter sounded once again and more grinning and clapping.

"Y que Gorzia," said one. "His name is García, teach!"

"All right, I'm sorry. Gar-cee-uh, what do I mean by the sounds of English."

García stood up, waited for the laughter to subside, and, hiding his impudence behind the pimples and blackheads on a face tanned by the sun, said: "The soun of English is . . ." and in Spanish, "the asshole of English!"

The new hail of guffaws and whistles finally cracked the porcelain face that had forced itself to hold together.

Champs

The cue made one more sweep over the green felt, hit the cue ball, and smacked it against the fifteen ball. The plump, yellowish hands remained still until the ball went clop into the pocket, and then they raised the cue until it was diagonally in front of his acned and fatuous face: his vaselined little curl fell neatly over his forehead, his cigarette was tucked jauntily behind an ear, his glance was oblique and mocking, and the fuzz on his upper lip had been accentuated with a pencil.

"Quiubo, man. Wha's up?" asked a sharp voice. "That was sure a champeen shot, eh?"

He started to laugh. His squat, pudgy body became a gaily trembling blob inside tight jeans and sweaty T-shirt.

He contemplated Gavilán—eyes once alive and now no longer so, three-day beard seeming to confound the ill humor on his face and not succeeding, long-ashed cigarette gripped between lips behind which swam curses—and enjoyed the feat he had perpetrated. He had won two games in a row. Of course, Gavilán had been in jail for six months, but that did not matter now. What mattered was that Gavilán had lost two games, and these victories placed him in a privileged position. They put him above the others, above the best players of the barrio, above those who had thrown the inferiority of his sixteen years, his childishness, in his face. No one now could deprive him of his place in Harlem. He was *el nuevo,* the successor to Gavilán and other respected individuals. He was equal . . . No. Superior, because of his youth: he had more time and greater opportunity to surpass all their deeds.

He felt like going out in the street and shouting: "I won two games in a row off Gavilán! Now say somethin, go ahead an say somethin!" He did not do it. He merely chalked his cue and told himself it wouldn't be worth it. It was sunny outside, but it was Saturday and the neighbors would be at the market at this hour of the morning. His audience would be snot-nosed kids and disinterested grandmothers. Anyhow, some humility was good in champions.

He picked up the quarter Gavilán had thrown down on the felt and exchanged a self-satisfied smile with the scorekeeper and the three spectators.

"Take wha's yours!" he said to the scorekeeper, wishing that one of the spectators would move to the other tables and spread the news, comment that he—Puruco, that fat kid, the one with the pimply face and the funny voice—had made the great Gavilán look ridiculous. But apparently those three wanted more proof.

He put away his fifteen cents and said to Gavilán, who was wiping the sweat from his face: "Wanna play another?"

"Sure," said Gavilán, picking another cue from the rack and chalking it meticulously.

The scorekeeper took down the triangle and set up for the next game.

Puruco broke, starting immediately to whistle and stroll elastically around the table, almost on the tips of his sneakers.

Gavilán approached the red ball with his characteristic heaviness and aimed at it, but he did not shoot. He simply raised his bushy head, his body leaning over the cue and the cloth, and said: "Lissen, quit whistlin.'"

"Okay, man," said Puruco, and swung his cue until he heard Gavilán's cue stroke and the balls rolled and cracked once again. Not one was pocketed.

"Ay bendito," laughed Puruco. "Man, I got this guy licked."

He shot at the one ball, made it and left the two ball lined up with the left pocket. The two ball made it also. He could not keep from smiling at all corners of the poolhall. He seemed to invite the spiders, the flies, the various numbers runners among the crowd at the other tables to witness this.

He studied the position of each ball carefully. He wanted to win this game too, to take advantage of his recent reading of Willie Hoppe's book and all those months of practice taunted by the mockery of his rivals. Last year he was no more than a little pisser; now real life was beginning, a champ's life. With Gavilán beat, he would defeat Mamerto and Bimbo . . . "Make way for Puruco!" the connoisseurs would say. And he would impress the owners of the poolhalls, he'd get good connections. He'd be bodyguard to some, intimate friend to others. He'd have cigarettes and beer for free. And women, not stupid girls who were always afraid and who wouldn't go further than some squeezing at the movies. From there to fame: the neighborhood macho, the man with a hand in everything—numbers, dope, the chick from Riverside Drive slumming in the barrio, the rumble between this gang and that to settle men's affairs.

With a grunt he miscued the three ball and swore. Gavilán was behind him when he turned around.

"Careful—doncha gimme the evil eye," he said bristling.
And Gavilán: "Aw, cuddid out."

"Naw, don' gimme that, man. Jus cause yer losin."

Gavilán didn't answer. He aimed at the red ball through
the smoke which was wrinkling his features, and shot,
pocketing two balls off opposite sides.

"See that?" asked Puruco, and he crossed his fingers to ward
off evil.

"Shut yer mouth!"

Gavilán tried to ricochet the five ball, but he missed.
Puruco studied the position of the ball and decided on the
farther but better lined-up pocket. As he was aiming, he
realized he would have to uncross his fingers. He looked at
Gavilán suspiciously and crossed his legs to shoot. He missed.

When he looked up, Gavilán was smiling and sucking his
upper gums, collecting bloody saliva to spit. Puruco no longer
doubted that he was the victim of an evil spell.

"Don' fool aroun, man. Play clean."

Gavilán looked at him surprised, stepping on his cigarette
distractedly.

"Wassa matter with you?"

"Naw," said Puruco, "don' go on with that *bilongo,* that evil
eye."

"Jeezus," laughed Gavilán. "He believes in witches!"

He brought the cue behind his waist, feinted once, and
pocketed easily. He pocketed the next. And the next. Puruco
got nervous. Either Gavilán was recovering his know-how or
that *bilongo* was pushing his cue. He had to step it up, or
Gavilán would win this game.

He chalked his cue, knocked on wood three times, and

waited for his turn. Gavilán missed his fifth shot. Then
Puruco set his range. He dropped the eight ball in. He did a
combination to pocket the eleven with the nine ball. Then the
nine made it. He cannoned the twelve ball into the pocket and
then missed on the ten ball. Gavilán also missed it. Finally
Puruco managed to make it, but for the thirteen ball he
almost ripped the felt. He added up. Only eight points
missing now, so he felt he could relax.

He moved the cigarette from his ear to his lips. As he was
lighting it with his back to the table so that the fan would not
blow out the match, he saw the scorekeeper's sly smile. He
turned quickly and caught Gavilán *in flagrante:* his feet were
off the ground and his body rested on the edge of the table to
make the shot easier. Before he could speak, Gavilán had
pocketed the ball.

"Lissen, man!"

"Watsa matter?" asked Gavilán calmly, eyeing the next
shot.

"Don' gimme that, kid! You ain gonna win like that!"

Gavilán raised an eyebrow to look at him and sucked in his
cheeks, biting the inside of his mouth.

"Wha's hurtin you?" he asked.

"No, not like that." Puruco opened his arms, almost hitting
the scorekeeper with his cue. He threw down his cigarette
violently and said to the spectators: "You saw'im, dinchya?"

"Saw what?" asked Gavilán, deadpan.

"That dirty move," shrilled Puruco. "You think I'm a
fool?"

"Aw jeezus christ," laughed Gavilán. "Don' ask me cause I
might tell you!"

Puruco struck the table edge with his cue.

"You gotta play clean with me. It ain enough you make magic first, but then you gotta cheat too."

"Who cheated?" asked Gavilán. He left his cue on the table and approached Puruco, smiling. "You tellin me I cheat?"

"No," said Puruco, his tone changing, his voice becoming childish, his body swaying. "But you shouldn' play like that, man. They seen you."

Gavilán turned to the others.

"Me cheat?"

Only the scorekeeper shook his head. The others said nothing, just looked away.

"But you was on top uh the table, man!" said Puruco.

Gavilán grabbed the front of his T-shirt almost casually, baring Puruco's pudgy back as he pulled him forward.

"Nobody calls me a cheat!"

At all the other tables the game had stopped. The others watched from afar. Nothing but the hum of the fan and the flies could be heard, and the shouts of the kids in the street.

"You think a pile uh shit like you can call me a cheat?" asked Gavilán, pushing into Puruco's chest with the fist that gripped his shirt. "I let you win two games so you could have somethin to brag about, and you think yer king or somethin. Geddoudahere, you miserable . . . ," he said between his teeth. "When you grow up I'll see you."

The shove pushed Puruco against the plaster wall, crashing him flat on his back. The crash snapped holes in the silence. Someone laughed, snickering. Someone said, "Wadda boaster!"

"An geddoudahere fore I kick yer ass," said Gavilán.

"Okay, man," stammered Puruco, letting the cue drop.

He walked out without daring to raise his eyes, hearing again the cue strokes on the tables, the little laughs. In the street he felt like crying but he didn't. That was sissy stuff. The blow he had received had not hurt him; what hurt was the other: "When you grow up I'll see you." He *was* a man. If they beat him, if they killed him, let them do it without considering his sixteen years. He was already a man. He could make trouble, lots of trouble, and he could also survive it.

He crossed to the other side furiously kicking a beer can, his hands in his pockets pinching the body nailed to the cross of adolescence.

He had let him win two games, said Gavilán. Liar. He knew that from now on he would lose all of them to him, the new champ. That's why the witchcraft, the cheating, the blow. Ah, but those three guys would spread the news of Gavilán's fall. Then Mamerto and Bimbo. No one could stop it now. The neighborhood, the whole world, would be his.

When the barrel stave tangled around his legs, he kicked it to one side and slapped the kid who came to pick it up.

"Wachout, man. I'll split yer eye."

And he went on walking, ignoring the mother who cursed him as she ran toward her crying child. He breathed deeply, his lips closed tight. As he moved along he saw streamers fall and heard cheers rain from the deserted and closed windows.

He was a champ. On his guard only for trouble.

Miniature 6

"An that trip, its gonna be to PR?"

The old woman looked again—this time with greater concentration—at the cards spread out on the table.

"Yes, to Puerto Rico, cause here I see palm trees."

"An will my kid love me when he grows up? It don' matter he's born like that?"

"Yer son always loved you," said the old woman with a honeyed smile. "Sons always love their mothers."

"Waddaya mean, always loved me? I'm only two months gone, an since Antonio and me we ain married . . ."

The old woman looked upset.

"Ah, but . . . Well, like I said, yer son's always loved you cause you been a real mother to that . . . husban of yours."

Sadness drained from the woman's face, making way for a flood of smiles.

God in Harlem

Her breasts were two painful mounds in the red sweater and her belly a passive volcano beneath the black taffeta skirt which only six months before had been her favorite party outfit. Leaning on the counter at El Iris Bar, she made circles with the wet glass, stopping from time to time to look at the clock above the mirrored shelf where the bottles were lined up.

"Hey, gimme another."

The waiter stopped mopping the floor and brought the bottle of Wilson's. He filled the shot glass and picked up the dollar the woman had been fingering distractedly. After bringing her change and wiping off the round stains on the counter, he went back to his mopping.

"Wachu up to, Nena?"

That thunderous voice reached her through the convulsions caused by the liquor. She put the empty glass on the bar, quickly blinked back her tears, and stood staring at the wall. She seemed to be demanding that the man project his image on the wall, so that she would not have to turn to see him put his foot on the rail. Then, as if she already saw his messy hair, his long sideburns, and his enormous double chin on the wall, she said:

"Bout time. I was gettin tired."

"Well, I almos didn' come," he said, smiling. He brought the slavered cigarette to his lips, then threw it away when he saw that it was out. "Since they tole me you was lookin for me to cut off my . . ."

She turned to look him up and down.

"I ain here to fool aroun, Microbio. You seem to think life's a joke."

"Nobody ain proved no different."

"Well, you got proof here," she said. "This is yours an you know it."

Moving away from the counter, she pointed to her body, a barrel without staves.

"Don' make me laugh, Nena, my lip's cut."

She tugged on her sweater to pull it over the deformed waistline and buttoned it, all the while looking at the man.

"One of these days somebody gonna cut it up for real," she said.

"Don' threaten me. You know what happens to me when people do that." Stiffening his neck in challenge, he almost looked as if he would bite her. But he immediately shrank back into disdain. "I start to shake, you see."

"You promised to help me," she cried. She lowered her voice when she realized that the few customers in the bar were listening. "After you got me when I was drunk an knocked me up, you said you'd . . ."

"What I tole you was I'd help you pay for the little job. But if you let all those months pass . . ."

He remained calm, not paying much attention to her, rapping his knuckles on the bar to call the bartender. As soon as he had ordered a beer she turned to him, her face distraught and shining like a new penny.

"Don' gimme that stuff cause it don' work all the time. Cause I don' wanna go aroun like Argelia with her ovaries an womb all outa place . . ."

"I could give a good shit about that," he said. He took his hand out of his pocket to toss a dime to the bartender.

"Coño, you know you did it in bad faith, Microbio. Pacache bet you couldn' knock me up an you . . ."

"Ah, Pacache tole you that? Well, let him take care of the kid. Anyhow, the five bucks I won off him didn' las long."

"Okay," she said. She raised her hand and moved it in a gesture of expectancy. "But jus remember that I'll get back at you."

"I tole you not to threaten."

Nena heard a violent click and felt a sharpness in her ribs. And before she dared look down, she knew it was a switchblade he had in his fingers.

"You better behave," said Microbio, hiding the weapon with the same sleight of hand he had used to take it out. He picked up the glass of beer and drank half of it down. "An if you gonna have a kid, you better look fer another job. If I knew how stupid you are, I wouldna bet."

For a moment he held the glass in the air as if he were demonstrating that the beer had evaporated and dared anyone to prove otherwise. Then he swallowed the rest, banged the glass down on the counter, winked at her as he wiped his mouth on the back of his hand, and walked out with his bow-legged swagger.

Nena remained, nervously rubbing the edge of the bar. She looked around for a glance of compassion, a gesture of understanding which would allow her to ask for help. But the painted women and the young men in baggy pants laughed and shouted without paying attention to her.

She asked for another whiskey and, fingers trembling, lit a cigarette. She was a stone rolling downhill. Not so, not even a stone, because her fear of abortion revealed her posture of imaginary strength. She was, simply, a clod of earth . . . rolling downhill. How could she get over the humps without crumbling to bits? The money she had saved for the trip to Puerto Rico—how many years since she had been there? five?—would hardly last until the delivery. Afterward she would have to get rid of the kid and put her life together again. But who would give it a home? The child of a whore. The only alternative was to abandon it on some stoop.

Easy to think it. She smiled with bitterness, once again making circles on the counter. To forget nine difficult months. To forget the somersaults in her belly. To forget that *that,* at least, had belonged to her. To forget that she could change paths. Be another woman: leave the dog's life of Harlem and devote herself to her child. Begin again, far from that devil Microbio.

She drank her whiskey deliberately. Fear still ran insane within her. The terror of a wound on her face. Involuntarily she remembered the tune and the words of that *plena:* "Cortaron a Elena, they cut up Elena . . ." She looked outside, fearing she would surprise Microbio hanging around. He was not there. Some men were leaning against the fenders of parked cars, watching for news of the lucky number in the clandestine Sunday drawing. On the opposite sidewalk people filed out of church, not crossing the avenue until they were far from the bar. Inside, the customers, realizing that eleven o'clock mass was over, began to play the jukebox.

She picked up her change, threw away her cigarette, and walked out the door, hiding her hands in the sleeves of her sweater. Once again she hated the city. She liked it in summer, when she could see it splashed with green. But not in autumn: not in the gray and cold enclosure smelling of dirty water. Not when it seemed to be the inside of an old metal washtub.

Two blocks down she heard the exclamations of the kids who walked toward her, and turned quickly, anticipating Microbio's attack. But behind her there were only surprised people looking and gesturing at the sheets of paper raining down. Some neighbors leaned out of the windows or went out onto the fire escapes trying to catch them.

Some reached her where she was standing. They were no more than white sheets, divided in half by a line of large, black letters which read in Spanish: AWAIT YE THE LORD. Looking at them indifferently, Nena raised her eyes toward the roofs where she expected to see people scattering them over the avenue. But she saw no one. And neither did she see the plane which could have been dropping them. The passersby had stopped to read and comment on the announcement. Curious, they looked around for the source of the sheets without finding it.

Turning the corner, Nena climbed the stoop of the first building she came to. The pane was cracked on the door she pushed open, and the walls of the hallway were peeling and chalk-scribbled: hearts and arrows, autographs and dirty words written in unschooled hand, deformed circles and lines and dots making the faces of unfinished figures. Behind the narrow and poorly lit staircase were piled dented garbage cans, varnished in grease and a residue of bones and papers.

On the second floor, taking the key from between her breasts, she opened the door marked 2D and ran to stretch out on the bed to calm her panting. Although it was noon the room was dark. Little light entered through the only window, which gave onto the fire escape. The room's dilapidation was distributed among a moth-eaten bed, two fragile chairs, a small, ramshackle dresser, and the worn and dirty linoleum.

"I hope God comes down an strikes the world with his fist an buries us all," she said to the plaster crucifix hanging over the bed. She was already beginning to feel nausea and a pain in her ankles.

She heard laughter and the voices of a man and a woman on the stairs. The sound of a key in the lock next door made her expectant. Hands slapping a backside in the midst of whispering, and the groan of the mattress minutes later, made her forget her indisposition. Suddenly she remembered the teacher: the man (the first one) who five years before had decided to discover her bountifully seductive body. That afternoon, the room closed after class, he had pretended to tutor her for the coming exam. She had anticipated the deed. And she had waited for him to gather the courage to take her. She had wanted finally, at seventeen, to acquire the sexual consciousness and competence which she envied in her married friends. She had wanted to clarify once and for all her diffuse notions about sex, notions which were the product of an endless stream of licentious jokes heard at women's parties and of persistent reading of the novels of Pedro Mata. That afternoon she had been the spider and the teacher an insignificant insect. When he sent her for the books she entered the cabinet looking for the proper corner in which to await him. And then, in the embrace, she had whispered her string of dirty words in order to compensate for the inferiority she always felt in his presence, in order to mock her own ingenuous ploy, in order to offer herself to him however, whenever, and wherever he wanted. She herself had raised her skirt, had fumbled for his belt and between his legs, attacking him, trying to shame him with her fierceness. And, ears alert to any strange noise outside the cabinet, eyes closed and lips bitten, she had perceived the clarity of her eyelids and the moan and delirium and happy giddiness of orgasm. He had plotted to be the spider, and she had deprived him of that role.

Now once again she heard laughter outside and she heard the couple go downstairs. And she thought that the sex act had never again provoked in her, nor would it, the happy confusion of that far-off afternoon.

"Maybe with jus one man," she said, "who won' be ashamed and who'll help me to change."

And she covered her face with the pillow, wanting to suffocate herself along with her frustration.

Friday night, no longer able to resist the desire for a drink, she went into El Iris. Microbio was swaying at the bar and she tried to go unnoticed to an empty table. But Microbio stopped shouting to the group gathered around him and went to sit with her.

"How's my Nena? Hey, lissen, I'm more bombed than a fly

in a pisspot. Well, I'm what they call loaded, and not with money."

He laughed without looking at her, and then, seeing her face still serious and anxious, he called the waiter.

"Two beers."

When the waiter moved away, Microbio took some coins from his pocket and put them on the table.

"Lissen, Nena, if you only knew that the fella you see servin there was a bum till a few days ago. But since he had a kid, or his wife had it, he's reformed. You don' believe the same thing can happen to me?"

"Yeah, sure. You real good for work."

"Come on, you don' believe I can go straight? Get this, that guy over there washes dishes in the daytime an waits on tables here at night. I can do the same thing. Don' tell me I can't."

Seeing that she didn't answer, that she merely stared at him, Microbio took out a pack of cigarettes and offered her one. She took it and waited for him to light it, trying at the same time to hide her nervousness. The musical din from the jukebox prevented her from hearing all of what he was saying, and for that reason she had to follow the jerky movements of his lips.

"Hey, Nena, how many more months you got?"

"Three."

"The kid better not turn out to be a pimp, cause the pimps union here is full up."

She remained expressionless, not allowing Microbio's words or his laughter to move her, smoking in silence.

"An the hospital?"

Nena flicked the ashes onto the floor and shrugged.

"That ain a problem," she said. "I'll wait till the las minute an then go to emergency."

"An afterward, wha happens? Cause I tole you. If you gonna raise him like that, you screwin an . . ."

She drew on the cigarette and exhaled all at once into the mocking eyes, then changed the cigarette to the other hand so that he would not realize that she had done it on purpose.

"If I wanna I can work in a factory."

"I was gonna say the same thing," said Microbio, moving his head up and down forcefully, as if he wanted to shake it off his shoulders. "Cause if you don', wha kinda example you gonna be fer the kid?"

Nena straightened in her chair and watched the waiter leave the bottles and the glasses on the table and pick up the correct change.

"Wassa matter with you now? Like you was my father."

"Its that I been bad," said Microbio, filling both glasses. "Its a weight on my conscience that the kid's gonna live like that. Unnerstan? Though I'm gonna tell you, I figured you'd get rid of it. I swear I thought . . . No, I'm gonna help you. But the minute . . . eh? . . . I split. The minute you get to be too much, I split."

"Okay, man, okay."

Nena threw the cigarette down and crushed it vehemently, letting out some of the joy which overflowed from inside of her. She felt like running to hug all the customers. She looked at Microbio again. She wanted to be sure that this was not just another trick.

"Hey, you wouldn' be tryin to fool me?"

"No, vieja." Microbio's face contracted, took on a martyred

expression. "You know that me, I . . . Any woman'd say yes to me, you know it. But us two can make a home fer that kid an . . ."

"Aw, don' come on with that. Take it slow, take it easy."

Seeing his face darken, Nena caressed the hand that twitched on the table.

"We'll do wha you wan, Microbio, but give it time."

"An ain I gonna see you?"

"Sure. But here."

"That all?"

"If you behave, then all you want," she said with a sly smile. "But I gotta try you out."

"Like we was engaged," he laughed.

"Like we was engaged," she laughed. And satisfaction flooded over her, and the world became a heap of dates and places and ordered acts.

Cheered by the clear sky which promised a warm Sunday, she settled down on a bench in Central Park to take the sun. She mistrusted Microbio's sudden transformation, but she relegated those thoughts to the farthest corner of her mind. Microbio wasn't bad. Microbio *wanted* to help her. And right now she needed more help, more advice, more support than ever. She was confused, fearful that she could not face the new life she was proposing to herself. Microbio *had* to be sincere. If not . . . what would become of her? A clod of earth rolling downhill . . . But with Microbio, all the problems of the future would be so much nonsense. And the moments of pleasant conversation and affection would be the smallest measure of a great happiness. God was watching over all three of them.

Seeing a group of boys approaching the lake, she thought of the children she would have one day. No doubt Microbio thought as she did: that in their children lay their own salvation. That they would have to work honorably for them. That they would have to change two lives in order to save others.

The boys were coming nearer now, following paper boats which, pushed by the wind, advanced toward her. When the boats bumped against the wall, their owners knelt by the water and put stones on the piles of papers they had under their arms. Then they gathered and lined up the boats for the next race. A foreboding made her look at the sheets of paper. They were identical, except for the text, to those of the previous Sunday. This time the line of large, black letters read in Spanish: THE LORD IS NIGH.

"Hey, where'd you get those papers?"

All of them looked up at the pregnant woman staring fearfully at the sheets.

"On Madison," said the oldest, raising his hand to give the go signal.

"Who from?"

The kid shrugged, gave the signal, and left with the others behind the boats.

Nena left the park hurriedly, and did not stop until she reached El Iris. The papers swirled madly on the corners.

"It's someone with nothin to do," she told herself.

Each time she thought of the inexplicable appearance of

the papers, she felt her heart beat uncontrollably. They crawled along the pavement. They whipped against the entrance of the poolhall or danced on the stoops of the buildings. She almost started to run, looking back at every moment to watch them jumping in the distance.

At the next corner she bumped into Microbio. He was wearing his green shirt and yellow tie, looking like a carnival puppet in the wrong place at the wrong time. Shaved, combed, smelling of cologne, he seemed someone else.

"I was lookin fer you to go to the movies, Nena. At the Boricua there's a good one."

"I don' feel so good. I'm gonna go lay down."

"Ah . . . Yuh wan me to bring you somethin from the drugstore?"

"Its jus things you get when yer pregnant."

"Okay, go lay down. I figured you'd like to go to the movies, but if yer sick . . ."

"Wait," said Nena, when Microbio began to move away. She thought of the enormous loneliness of her small room, of her fear of the sheets of paper, of her need to chat with someone to forget them. "Come an les talk some."

In the room she motioned him to a chair and went to straighten the messy bed. Then she opened the window to evict the smell of dust and sleep. There were men kneeling on the stoop across the way, crowded around a pile of bills and coins. One of them was saying something unintelligible while he listened to the sound of the dice in the hollow of his hand. When he threw them against the wall, he closed his fist and cursed.

"I bet no one'll know how to pray when He comes."

"What?"

Turning, she faced Microbio, who was sitting astride the chair, his arms resting on its back.

"Those papers, I bet its true that God's about to come."

"Aw, cuddid out," he gesticulated. "You get fooled by any little thing. Watch out you don' pull a Mary Magdalen on me."

"Don' gimme Mary Magdalen!" Crossing the room, Nena went to stretch out on the bed, on her back, making a pillow of her arms. "I don' go to church, but I believe in God."

When she felt the movement in her belly, she began to rub it.

"Tha's like everybody," said Microbio. "I got my religion too."

He saw her bulging in the shadow, waving her legs in the air, her skirt moving with her hand and bit by bit uncovering her thighs.

"Ay, if I could only have this kid soon."

He got up, removing the chair from between his legs and putting it to one side.

"It hurt?"

"Naw, but I think I got gas. An then this kid kicks so much."

"You wan me to give you a rubdown?"

"If you do it careful, yeah. The witchazel's on the dresser."

Microbio brought the bottle and settled down next to her. With one hand he unbuttoned her sweater and pulled her blouse from under the skirt. And then he pulled down her skirt and panties enough to expose the englobed flesh and the protruding navel. Nena shivered on feeling his damp hand on her belly. She closed her eyes and stretched her arms back, adding a slight sway to her body as it was rocked by Microbio's hand. She was scratching at the sheet and moving her hips more rhythmically when she heard the bottle fall to the floor. She thought of stopping Microbio, she thought of running out of the room, but she did nothing. He was settling his noisy breath against her eyelids and nothing else mattered.

She awoke to organ music and the patter of rain on the fire escape. She groped at her side for the naked body which was no longer there. Then she sat up in bed and waited for her eyes to adjust to the dark. The organ music was abruptly interrupted. Static and voices in English took its place randomly for a moment, until the hand which was turning the knob in a neighboring room stopped. Now a mambo played, got louder, and remained to shake and sway the atmosphere.

She finally made out the chairs. She lay back when she realized that Microbio's clothes were gone. Thinking about him, she remembered the past week: days and nights full of swaggering and moans and surprise attacks. She wanted life to go on like that, no more than one long, meaningful sex act. Only one man to bring an end to her loneliness. Only one body. Only one voice.

She wanted him on top of her again, listening to the sound of rain. In the midst of uninterrupted organ music, in the midst of radio sermons. In the midst of a rainy Sunday like this one, which needed only to see and hear them make love in order to clear up.

She stretched. For a moment she was distracted by the ticking of the alarm clock. She did not feel like getting up, yet she was hungry. If Microbio would only come back soon with coffee and a sandwich . . . She got out of bed listlessly and turned on the light. The clock said past eleven. No wonder she was hungry. She rolled up the window shade. If only it would stop raining. Still drowsy, she put on the red sweater and the taffeta skirt. She promised herself once again that that very afternoon she would fix up some dresses. The skirt no longer fastened, could not be let out anymore, and had lost its sheen.

In the bottom drawer of the dresser she looked for the olive jar where she kept her savings. Taking out a fifty cent piece, she noticed that the contents had diminished considerably. She did not remember having spent that much. Unless . . . Microbio!

Taking an old newspaper to shield herself from the rain, she went out into the street.

"Seen Microbio?"

No one at the poolhall said he had. Some shook their heads disinterestedly. Others said no, but smiled, looking at her belly. They turned to chalk their cues or lean over the cue balls on the green felt, without saying any more.

"Seen Microbio?"

At El Iris, the few customers looked at her in silence.

"He ain been aroun here," said one. "What? You still ain dropped that kid?" He laughed, looking at the others.

She got the feeling that they were all plotting something against her, something that went beyond denying that Microbio had been with them some time before.

"Who'd Microbio bet with this time?"

The man feigned seriousness.

"What bet?"

"Don' worry," she said. "I'll fin out."

In the street once again, she stayed under the bar's awning, waiting for the rain to let up. People were coming out of church, clutching their missals like shields.

Suddenly the papers started to drop like slaps, beating on umbrellas and parked cars. People stopped without knowing what to do, without speaking, without even daring to look at the papers which were disintegrating in the rain.

The priest came out onto the sidewalk. His angry face looked out from under an umbrella and his chubby pink hand gestured with authority.

"Walk, walk," he said to the people. "I've already told you that this is the Devil's work."

A man with a broom followed him, on his orders hurriedly sweeping the papers toward the river which flowed down-gutter. The people moved into groups of three and four to share umbrellas and walked rapidly away.

Nena looked on the roofs to see who was scattering the papers. And did not find them. The papers had come as if from some catapult into the rectangular emptiness of the avenue. Heedless of the rain, she crouched slowly to pick one up. It was another large, black-lettered notice in Spanish, longer this time: THE LORD WILL BE AMONG US NEXT SUNDAY, 11 A.M. 114 ST. & MADISON AVE.

It was as if she had been pierced by an electric shock. She dropped the paper and started to run in the downpour, without seeking refuge under awnings, stopping for only a moment in the doorway of her building to catch her breath.

Then she ran upstairs, through the door of her room, and fell to her knees on the bed in front of the crucifix. In her mind she was still running and closing doors and looking for a way out of the labyrinth through which Microbio was chasing her. She could never get away if God did not help her. Microbio's transformation, she now understood, was no more than a plot to kill the baby. God had to save her from his deceit.

"I won' sin no more," she said. "You can see me an you know I wanna change."

Praying, she had a vision of an old film she had seen so many times during Holy Week in her hometown: a shameless, half-naked woman passed through the village on a luxurious chair carried by some Negroes. Later, submissive and prematurely old, she kissed and washed with her tears the feet of Him who had pardoned her. And finally she was no more than a purified face, tearfully raised toward the cross on which hung the frail, slack body which would refuse to remain underground.

The banging on the door frightened her. Crossing herself quickly, she went to open it.

"Wa's goin on here?"

Before she could react, Microbio entered unsteadily, shouldering her aside, waving an almost empty bottle.

"A little drink, Nena."

She closed the door and went to sit on the bed, next to her fear.

"You began so early."

"You wanna little drink?"

"No."

"Here's to what I got an you aint," said Microbio. He tilted the bottle, swallowing noisily, and then threw it under the bed.

"Wachu come here for, Microbio, to steal sommore?"

"But I'll pay you back," he said, moving toward her. "I always pay what . . ."

Nena ran to the door when he tried to embrace her.

"Wassə matter with you?" asked Microbio. "Doncha like me no more?"

"I'm tired of yer shit. So, geddouda here!"

He was swaying next to the bed, smiling sloppily.

"An I'm gonna tell you somethin," said Nena. "I'm gonna have this kid fer better fer worse."

"An whose saying you can't have it?"

"I figured out yer little game, Microbio."

"You crazy," he said, throwing himself on the bed, face up.

"You better leave now."

"Who says, God?"

"From now on yer gonna see how things change."

"An if I go, how you gonna get yours then? Come on, you know yer religion's right between my legs."

Nena took off one shoe and hobbled to the bed.

"Geddouda here, you bastard, or yer gonna get it."

Microbio leaned on his elbow, seeing above him the fish mouth, the sharp mouth ending in a reddish point.

"You wouldn' dare, Nena."

"Geddout!"

"I betcha you won' do it!"

Nena raised the shoe and struck the head, which fell

forward, shook itself, and raised again, opening angered eyes. Immediately she felt one hand gripping her throat and the other struggling with the hand which held the shoe.

The blood rushed to her face and her body wavered from a drunken and enraged shove. When she stumbled and fell against the wall, her head became a bloody hammer in Microbio's hands. Again she struck the shapeless form which was almost on top of her, and then she felt the heel break, while her face still came and went with his slaps.

Once out of the vertigo, she found herself under the compassionate look of the neighbors who were trying to stop her endless scream. And only then did she stop beating against the floor with the useless sole, in order to cough and spit the phlegm that was choking her.

Through her crying she saw the men file out. She let herself be undressed by the women before she collapsed moaning on the bed. And while someone ripped the sheet to bandage her head, and others began to bathe her with witch hazel, she gripped her belly to make sure it had not caved in.

Brick dust was blowing from the abandoned buildings, and in a corner of an empty lot a pile of garbage burned. Kids in wide-brimmed hats and baggy pants kept their hands in their pockets and stamped on the ground to drive away the cold. In front of them, above the breath converted into little vapor clouds, they could see a man standing on a pile of broken bottles and rotted wood, and an anemic women standing next to an American flag.

Nena joined the crowd, which continued to grow despite

the cold and cloudy day. Her black fuzzy jacket, straining its buttons, was torn on both sides. And her eyes were no more than cracks in her bluish face.

Her credo of superstitions had convinced her that today there would be a catastrophe. Today she and the world which she hated so would collapse. Evil would disappear: this consoled her. Now she prayed in silence, thinking about the child who, since the beating, had stopped its movements in her belly. Thinking how different everything would have been if only she could have given birth.

"Listen, brother!" shouted a man in the crowd. "When does the Lord appear? Man, I'm gettin numb."

There, in front, the preacher whispered to one of his companions and she handed him a book with red edges.

"Aw, don' give us what we already know," said an old woman.

"Oh, you wretches!" bellowed the man in Spanish, after returning the book and raising his arms to the heavens.

"Carajo, if you gonna insult us . . ."

"Brothers!" said the man.

"Finish, chico, finish. We gonna be here all day."

"The Lord," said the man, "who sees everything and hears everything, won' come so long as there's so many sinners on Earth."

"What Earth? Doncha mean mud?"

As the laughter increased, the preacher stretched his arms toward them.

"Abandon the paths of perdition!" he warned.

"Aw, cuddid out!"

Nena understood now what was wrong with this spectacle.

There would be no thunder, no lightning, no sound of harps, no celestial voices. The world would not crumble, nor would Evil disappear from amongst them. Like herself, everyone had come as to an empty cage where they hoped to see a freak. And it was stupid.

But *they* remained safe in their evil. Only she was losing a world: her hope. Because there was nothing more for her to do. Her child was lost, so she was lost. Tomorrow did not exist. Only the inferno of her loneliness, the continuation of an adventure begun five years before. For another woman it would have been no more than a risk, an impulsive adolescent act that with cunning could have remained a pleasant accident. She, however, had perpetuated the adventure, squandering and debilitating her impulsiveness. She had distorted risk itself.

"Hear the Lord's word, brothers, before it's too late!" said the man. "Don't insist on following Satan's path."

"Naw, wha happen is that nobody'd sell the Lord a plane ticket to come here!"

The guffaws became louder each time someone in the back let out a whinny. Then scattered voices began to intone a song:

"Manda fuego, Señor, manda fuueegoooo!"

The man stopped preaching and took the book to read from it. Perhaps to get strength from the passage itself. Perhaps to raise a wall between the mockery and himself.

"If I'd of known this, I would of stayed in bed," said one, leaving the crowd.

"Wait fer me," said his companion. "Les go to the bar an get some holy water."

They were followed by complete dispersion: children ran,

pushing each other, and women followed behind them, admonishing them not to cross the street, while the men came last, imitating their screeching voices and their waddles.

Nena's voice stopped them for an instant.

"God is here!"

Tense, eyes closed, her face raised as if to sniff the dry air, she caressed her belly as she swayed.

"Jeezus, that one's gettin all hot an bothered," someone said. "Why, if what she got there's the holy ghost, then my wife's got a church!"

She heard neither laughter nor comments. All she heard was the voice coming from afar: "I am the door: he who passes through me will be saved . . ."

And feeling her belly, she murmured: "God-is-here God-is-here God-is-here . . ."

She knew neither pain, nor hate, nor bitterness. She was being born.